Hungry Ghost

A Collection of Poetry About Self-Harm and Self-Love

Aspen Harvey

TRIGGER WARNING

The following content could be triggering for people dealing with anxiety and depression. If you struggle with suicidal thoughts, please contact the National Suicide Prevention Lifeline 1-800-273-8255.

This book in no way promotes suicide, self-harm, or abuse. I want the following content to be a transparency of emotions that any individual can deal with.

DEDICATION

To Richard Braithwaite and Jaime Johnson for believing in me when I didn't believe in myself and to those of you who struggle with self-harm. Wear your scars without shame: you have intense emotions, do not feel guilty and do not apologize.

CONTENTS

EPIGRAPH

Let's go someplace where no one knows our names
And no one cares that we've had others.

UNTITLED LIFE

Fingers chunky and clumsily clutching at the side of the
pool.
Water: a crisp blue, an ironed blue, a picture-perfect blue.
Ribbons of summer sunlight shining across the ripples that
surround me.
Cherry life jacket hiked up, ears: swallowed whole.

Black straps across my chest, tight breaths are all I manage.
The world is a dark gray, or at least appears to be through
my bright yellow goggles.
Life had so much colour back then.
The blues, the reds, the yellows… even my skin seems
pinker than it is now.
Not even sure if I was aware a photo was being taken; face
scrunched up to keep the goggles from slipping or maybe
squinting against the sunlight.

My dad was probably crouched near the edge,
camera gripped tightly to keep it from falling in the water,
the gap between two of his side teeth apparent while lip
pulled up
in concentration and from the effort of winking to see
through the eyepiece.

This is the beginning, he thinks.
This is where it starts.
She will be a swimmer like me and her mom.
I'll spend weekends teaching her fly and driving her to meets.

Mom was probably thinking along similar lines, with of
course the occasional,
"Aw. My gawwwd, she's so cute."
How disappointed they must be.
Coached for 15 years and now: too scared to step in a pool
without shorts
(scars turn purple when cold and therefore become more
evident underwater).
They don't know that though.
They probably just think that they pushed me over the
edge.

They were so busy instructing me on how to move my
arms and legs and how to breathe
that they didn't notice how they'd step on my fingers,
clenched over the side of the pool.
They think I've been pushed over the edge and that they're
responsible.
Put too much pressure on swimming, academics, reading,
socialization, and life.

Not enough focus on what *I* want.

It's been so long of this that I don't know what I wanted.

What I want now.

My psychiatrist says I'm underdeveloped mentally.

That although I'm 17, I'm at the developmental age of a

15-year-old.

She says that I need to figure who I am. I don't know who

I am.

I REMEMBER...

I remember the flowers I'd eat on the playground.

I remember climbing down a mountain, mouth full of mist.

I remember lying awake in bed. I remember cupping my breasts in the dark. I remember my ears ringing from the phantom chop, I'd imagine the things my parents would say when they woke in the morning and saw the gardening shears, saw the blood.

I remember scooping snails off the sidewalk during recess.

I remember how she laughed at my body. I remember the first time I thought I was fat.

I remember how the mouse's spine snapped. I remember how tightly the bird's beak was clasped around the torso. The entrails smeared or sandwiched between slats of wood.

I remember a turtle laying eggs, I remember kissing her shell.

I remember striking a match, blowing it out and pressing it into my thigh.

I remember building a stone circle in the forest.

I remember the rough sandstone on my wrist, the beams of head lamps surveying the dunes, the faint call of my name. The mumbling from my lips. I remember shaking with the question: *am I going insane?*

I remember that same sandstone against the skin of my back early in the morning. How the winds licked my sweat dry. I remember crows circling above and my nipples hard in the cold.

I remember how tightly I gripped the hammer above my splayed fingers. I remember the rasp of breath under the rope. I remember feeling like my face was about to burst like a swollen berry pinched between finger and thumb.

I remember hiking through a petrified forest where all the trees were showcased in dugout graves.

. . . .

I remember when my parents tried to coax me to venture with them into a cave known for its swarms of bats. My mom told me I'd be a fool to miss it, that it was a once in a lifetime experience, but all I really wanted to do was swing in a hammock and be seen by my sister.

I remember reading over his shoulder, the words he'd scribbled down. The letters hastily jammed together, jostling and elbowing each other for space, it was a struggle to pull them apart. Once I did, I realized that he'd written a paragraph about the shadows around my eyes and how he blushed thinking about his favorite birthmark of mine. I remember the page he wrote about how my nose crinkled when I'd smile.

I remember when I was in love. I remember when I was alone. What I can't recall is whether I was more in love with the loneliness or with you.

. . . .

NINE WAYS OF LOOKING AT A SCAR

I.

Stepping over roots
I look up, the boughs with scars above
Ingrained in bark, dance.

II.

The way the image of the
Rope dangles in my mind's eye
Tightens around my throat, thoughts
Of how scarred I am.

III.

Deer caught in the headlights,
I can't look anymore.
Why do
The scars
Sing?

IV.
The earth trembles, splits.
Fossilized history spews
Ribbons of loose sediment.

This earth is broken.
The land is scarred beyond hope.
Reduced to craters.

V.
Crisscross of purple
Splayed like ferns, the scars wrap
Around her backbone.

Pulling her down and
Supporting her heart,
The way their words never could.

VI.
Baby skin soft as
White porcelain, the type I
Could never lay eyes
On for fear my heart
Would break. Mine: ravaged and scarred.

VII.
The rocks have been scarred, stripped of moss and skin
Laying under the blistering sunlight
Begging to be cleaved in half… a miracle.

VIII.
The lamb's eye under
The slaughter, weeping
Tears of mock indifference

I know how the meat
Will taste: scorched and scarred.

IX.
A sleeve can only hide so
Much. The pain bristles under
Thin white scars. Don't look.

THE TREE THAT BROKE

Black ink drips from my teeth,
pools in the hollows of my cheekbones
you tell me: smile, please smile
but I can't—
I trip over hammocks and picnic tables.
My feet are shells, broken and thrown
in the wink and wave.
ACDC guitar strap wrapped around
their slender neck, swinging from a
dilapidated treehouse, consumed by termites.
The beams barely hold them.
He prays: just a little longer.
I choke on the blackness bubbling through me.
I want to scream, I want to yell,
get out, get out of here.
He takes them by the hand and I
break, mouth too full of moaning
to tell him all the things he should not know.

There's just one thing in my life that I can't live with.

- me

. . . .

NO CONTROL

Don't tell me I'm not in control.
The blade settles into my palm with ease.
I control everything.
How much would you like it to hurt tonight?
I just need it to sting.
How much would you like it to bleed?
An angry seepage, a slow overflow, enough to stain your
pants,
To drip down your leg?
Would you like that cut medium or rare. Juicy?
I can do it all
Don't tell me I'm not in control.

THE CHICKEN WAS BORN TODAY

He picked up a baby chicken,
Placed her in the palm of my hand,
Gave me a mushed grape
And the assurance that
I was doing everything alright.
Ha.
If I was "doing everything alright"
I wouldn't be jabbing a paper clip into my hand
To make the loneliness stopstopstop--
If I was "doing everything alright"
I wouldn't be cussing at my reflection in the mirror
Wishing I was fucking different.
Why can't I just love myself?
If I was "doing everything alright"
He wouldn't have sat me down in the cemetery and
broken my heart.
He wouldn't have left me for 45 minutes sitting there,
swaying in the wind and sudden emptiness.
If I was "doing everything alright"
I'd have told my mom how I've hated, no, *despised* my
body for
Six. Years.
I've been rationalizing it since, blaming my dysphoria on
my best friend
(at the time)

Who bullied me, making snarky comments on how I was
maturing… but my psychiatrist said,
It's not normal to daydream about chopping your breasts off
with gardening shears,
dear.
I asked my mom if I'd be ready for college,
Ready to live by myself.
She said she'd *liiiiiike* it if I weren't dependent on
medication.
She treats my mental health like it's something that will go
away
That I can go back to being *me* again.
Doesn't she know: *I d o n ' t k n o w* how to go back.
My psychiatrist asked me: *if I could take away the self-harm*
with a snap of my fingers, would you want that?
I I I I I would want to lunge and pin down her hands and
yell NONONONONO
Because I don't know who I am without it.
I don't know how to BE without it.
If I was "doing everything alright"
I would be confident and stride up to the boy in the
jellyfish T-shirt
And whisper into his ear that he's funny and cute and I
like his style*music*poetry.
If I was "doing everything alright"
That goddamn bird wouldn't have shat in my hand.

DEAR MOM AND DAD

If I ever find the strength to say all the things I want to say
to you,
I hope you don't get in my way.
It's been too long, too terrible, too unbearable.
Let me speak.
No, I don't want to hear your voice, I'm tired of your
interruptions.
LISTEN TO ME.
Shut up for two seconds, so I can tell you
All the things I hate about myself.
Fuck you, stop explaining your side of the story.
I've read that part already; my side isn't written yet.
Give me the pen; stop stealing the paper.
Let me speak and write down all the parts of myself I wish
you never made.
I don't care about all the great things you love about me,
Those are the parts I hate.
Learn to love my voice instead of my body.
WILL YOU LET ME SPEAK?
For crying out loud: *let me cry out loud*
Instead of burrowing my face into the soggy pillow,
sinking my teeth trying not to be heard.
You'll come in with your words ready to drown out my
pain.
Don't you understand, I want the pain.

. . . .

I want to feel heard, not loved.
I want to be loved- stop listening to me- I DON'T
KNOW WHAT I'M SAYING
I don't know how to ask for help.
Don't you get it?! I don't know what I want, so shut the
fuck up.
The more you say you love me, the more I think you're
just saying it.
Not *meaning* it. I want to be meant.
I want to mean something.
I want to feel like I am worth meaning.
Something that doesn't mean anything is nothing.
I don't want to be nothing anymore.
I want to mean.

HOW TO PARENT PAIN

Stumbling on a book: How to Parent
Teenagers with Intense Emotions.
Its cover, glossy, reflecting my dad behind me.
He utters abashedly: "It's homework"
like he's taking a class he'll pass or fail.
Like he's cramming for the exams before it's too late.
We don't talk about it and I've ruffled through every
drawer not finding it again.
I just want to see if his writing is on the pages. If he's taken
notes.

REGRET

My only regret
Was sleeping with the light on.
Now I'm lost in dark.

FLASHLIGHT

Beaming at me, that smile like
Headlights screaming into bitten palms
Flash flash flash
Claws raking my flesh.
Ribbons choking my neck.
Hanging, I can feel it getting closer
Flash flash flash
Fist around my lungs
Footsteps- are you real- in my head.
Flash flash flash
Seizing muscles,
Head rocking on pillow—
Are you reaching out
Flash flash flash
Or reaching in?
Underwater lullabies.
Slime against my thigh
Flash flash flash
Coming, it's coming it's
Flash flash flash
Here it is
Flash flash flash
!!!
          light.

LAST NITE

Tell me about last night.
My throat tightens.
Last night?
Yeah, you've mentioned it a couple of times, can you tell me
what happened?
I don't want to.
Take your time.
Bedsheets strewn in crumpled heaps.
The way my hand claws at my scabs, itching for release,
I want to cry.
Heaviness behind my eyelids, teetering over the edge
Why can't I cry?
There's humming from the closet.
I close my eyes shaking my head vigorously
No no no nonono--
I wasn't myself.
Who were you?
Some- somebody else.
Fingers tickle the shoelaces, ends dangling, a knot pulled
taunt,
Kneecaps slipping off the stool.
Have you ever tried to, uh...
No. Maybe. I don't know. I haven't but, that other person...
they have. A few times.
Last night?

· · · ·

Yeah.

Grasping breath, the way the face swells red and then
purple
Eyes wide, frightened, about to burst
POP!
What's that?
Huh? Oh, uh, nothing. I don't know how to talk about it.
That's alright, do you mind if I ask you a few questions?
No, no that's okay.
Alright. How often?
Slamming computer screen, chest capsizing
Collapsing *i can't breathe*
Every night.
Are you safe? With yourself.
I don't trust myself anymore, not after what they've done to
me.
What did they do to you?
Terrible things. I don't know how to talk about it.
Chord pinching neck
Sucking sounds, vision splotchy
Fading, fading in and out in and
Are you in pain?
Killmekillmekillme why can't I kill myself?
I don't want to die.

I'VE GOT NOTHING UP MY SLEEVE

Lift up your sleeve.
Lifts up sleeve.
Let me have a look.
Grabs wrist and pulls arm closer.
What's wrong with you?
Pulls arm back, shakes sleeve back in place.
Huh?! Why have you cut up your arm like that?
Head lowered, ashamed, scared, speechless.
What do you have to say for yourself?
"I just want to feel real again."

LISTENING TO MUSIC IN THE LIBRARY

A pair of oversized headphones
slipping their way off
my ears.

The edge
of your shoe
kissing mine.

The way your fingers toy
the turtle ring off
my pinky and
graze the spot
on my left hand that's a little
W r O n G
a little
B r O k E n.
I imagine pulling up
my sleeve, fabric hairs
catching on still-wet scabs
weeping at the seams
can you see how I'm

F
  A
      L
      L
      I
      N
      G
apart?
Your expression changes
as you see
what I did yesterday.
My skin is cracking,
F
  A
      L
      L
      I
      N
      G
off.
Red hurt pulses within
I just want it
outoutoutoutoutout
GET THE FUCK OUT
of my body.
I want to feel real again--

What happened to the kid,
spongy cheeks sagging
with sobs, spit, and hard
breath?
Blades
       scissors
           paper
clips keep them together now,
all my frayed pieces.
No need for messy
sadness
(are you okay? - yeah I'm fine, smile).
Open the drapes, let it all
leave through
tiny red windows,
dark stained sills
ingrained with the pain.

I need you
and a teal blanket with
white words of positivity (literally,
you know the one).

. . . .

I need blurry eyes,
a heartbreaking tragedy
playing from a computer. Mostly,
I just need
your arms
around my broken ones
while I cry and cry and
cry.

I push the headphones
back into place
and
move my foot away
from yours.

I squeeze the
paperclip in
my pocket.

. . . .

ME&U

Look at me.
Look forward to seeing me, look past me, look through
me.
Cry out to me. Cry instead of me.
Greet me, eat me, enjoy me.
Go insane for me.
Celebrate me, rejoice me, yell at me.
Open your legs and swallow bullets for me.
Cast aside old lovers and discard their wilting skins for me.
Imagine me.
Create me.
Define me.
Quiet me, shit me, drink me, consume me.
Laugh at me, spit at me, throw rocks at me, forget me.
Free me.
Pretend to be someone else with me. Pretend to be me.
Pretend no one's watching but me.
Pretend you know me.
Pretend you love me.
Pretend that you want to love me.
Kill for me, kill me.
Kill the thing inside of me.
You are me.
He is me.
She is me.

. . . .

Fuck me.

Write the rest of my life for me, live instead of me, die for me, die with me.

Be the one who dies because of me.

Dress me, undress me, chop off your tongue for me.

Kick me, hurt me, push me.

Keep me, treasure me, cherish me.

Adore me, kiss me, tell me about how lonely you were before you met me.

Hoard me, hide me.

Hesitate when talking about me.

Forget to breathe when around me.

Replace me, return me, attempt to rationalize me.

Understand me, see me, separate me.

Separate yourself from me, do whatever you want with me.

I don't want me.

I don't want you.

I do whatever I want with you, separate myself from you.

Separate you, see you, understand you.

Attempt to rationalize you, return you, replace you.

Forget to breathe when around you.

Hesitate when talking about you.

Hide you, hoard you.

Tell you about how lonely I was before I met you, kiss you, adore you.

Cherish you, treasure you, keep you.

· · · · ·

Push you, hurt you, kick you.

Chop off my tongue for you, undress you, dress you.

Be the one who dies because of you.

Die with you, die for you, live instead of you, write the rest
of your life for you.

Fuck you.

She is you.

He is you.

I am you.

Kill the thing inside of you.

Kill you, kill for you.

Pretend that I want to love you.

Pretend I love you.

Pretend I know you.

Pretend no one's watching but you.

Pretend to be you. Pretend to be someone else with you.

Free you.

Forget you, throw rocks at you, spit at you, laugh at you.

Consume you, drink you, shit you, quiet you.

Define you.

Create you.

Imagine you.

Cast aside old lovers and discard their wilting skins for
you.

Open my legs and swallow bullets for you.

Yell at you, rejoice you, celebrate you.

Go insane for you.

· · · ·

. . . .

Enjoy you, eat you, greet you.
Cry instead of you. Cry out to you.
Look through you, look past you, look forward to seeing
you.
Look at you.

. . . .

. . . .

FROZEN

Water rushing down my throat,
Tensing, freezing, expanding.
Inner muscles contracting, straining
Shards of glass-like ice piercing red flesh
The insides exploding.
I want to blow up,
Shatter into a million pieces
So that no matter how hard they try,
I'll never be put back together again.

. . . .

shoelaces,
a closet,
clothes
pushed
to one
side,
a knot.

- you know the rest

I HAVE NOTHING TO APOLOGIZE FOR

He says my poetry is repetitive.
A yawn: oh this again.
I'm sorry my pain is continuous.
I'm sorry my suffering is a bore to you.
I'm sorry my self-hatred is a vicious cycle
Of deprecation and negative self-talk.
I'm sorry these words don't come as a shock
To you anymore. Forgive me, for they still
Steal my breath and leave me speechless.
I don't write to keep you entertained.
I write so that I don't go rummaging in my room for
Something remotely sharp or pointed to
Jab into my skin.
I write so that these ghosts in my head don't
Devour me whole.
I write so that I don't forget who I am
When my hands are stained red and I can't
Remember what it is I've done to myself.

I ATE DANDELION SEEDS

It was a long time ago. You wouldn't remember. But.

As a girl, I ate dandelion seeds. I would finger the fuzzy heads and giggle as their flocculent tips tickled the inside of my nose. I'd cup a single seed with both hands squeezed airtight and hold my breath, make a wish. Sometimes, if I really wanted my wish to come true, I'd crawl under my blankets in bed and murmur my wish seven times, waiting three seconds between each whisper for extra luck. And then, making sure no one was around, I'd delicately place the seed on the tip of my tongue with a tilted head and swallow my little wish carrier. It was all jokes to you, but I took pride in my many wishes. I wished ferociously that you'd hold my hand, trace my cheek bones with your gentle forefinger, maybe even kiss my lips. You'd make fun, eyes twinkling with tease. Kick my pile of dandelions, sneer, "What are these?" But at night, I would imagine the seeds gliding down my throat and feel them fluttering against the inside of my skin to settle at the base of my tummy, little roots springing forth, wiggling to find purchase within. Feeble stalks thicken, grow bold. The petals: velvety, stems covered in small hairs. I'd fall asleep smiling with my arms curled around my belly. My wishes grew into a little garden.

· · · ·

Things, now, have changed. Too often, my knuckles whiten as they clutch the rattling bed frame. Your starved fingers shove their way between my thighs and tear at the roots of my being. Ravenous teeth bite at the petals and you don't even bother chewing with your mouth closed. Spittle flies. My breath hitches as your tongue, thick and slimy, hooks around flowers and breaks spines. Blood pours from the snapped stems but I keep my thighs clenched until you leave, shredded bouquet in hand. You scoff on your way out, "What are these?" My empty stomach trembles. The door slams. My legs, wet. The bed, soaked. Petals, strewn everywhere. Wilty and dead, I find them in my hair, slathered upon my breasts.

Days later, I am surprised to find some still twisted in the bed sheets where you raked me raw. All day I lay with my back against the cold wall and my hands clutch at what was once there, while your ghost lips continue to suck on my wrinkled flesh. I am barren. Nothing grows here anymore. I resort to choking down handfuls of dandelion seeds. I jump fences, steal into backyards and snatch up seedlings, flowers, leaves too. Never are my pockets vacant. I dive for stray seeds growing in cracked sidewalks, hoard them in the backs of drawers, under the mattress. I stuff myself until my stomach is brimming with fluffy emptiness and seeds are spilling from my lips and I

wait for you
to come back to bed.

· · · ·

MESS ON THE FLOOR

Zipping up my coat, I'd like to keep
these secrets from you.
Lips glued, smacking with the aftertaste
Of love, can you feel the sticky want I have to
S

      P

          I

             L

                L

disastrous memories upon the floor?
Open my mouth with scarred hands,
let them seep into the carpet, dear.
It's my mess, not yours.

. . . .

WHATEVER HAPPENED TO US? DIDN'T I LOVE YOU?

Toss all your thoughts to the sea.
Let's get lost in the waves.
There's no need for sound here.
Let your mind quiet down,
Numbing all those mazes in your head
But don't leave me.

There's something special,
Something secret between two people
And the silence that fills the space
From my mouth to yours.
But when you go, that contentment
Bubbles up towards the surface,
I sink, sink, sink with the quiet.

I know you can't help how things are,
How things have been these last
Few years, but there's an ocean
Here. No matter how deep I go,
My loneliness has no end.
I miss you.

. . . .

I miss the way your feet would rub
Against each other under the covers
While I read from a book.

I miss the times you'd sneeze.
And sneeze again.
And again.
All the things that got me hot with
Annoyance, I now crave.
Why did you have to go away?

My fingers itch. Twitch. Squirm
With paper clips or pieces of twine
To avoid checking my phone again.
You never talk any more.

I miss your voice. Your fingers on
The acoustic. Your lips on the horn.
How you'd bite the pen caps and then
Jump as they broke just to settle back in
With another pen.

We had something no one else did.
I think I knew you in my dreams.
You were the one wearing a trench coat
That swirled above the pavement
Above planets and revolving galaxies.

You were the one I caught in the glass jar
On that island just beyond the tumbling forest.
Wings a little tattered and torn, eyes big and heavy.
You had come such a long way and didn't know at the
time
How much farther you would have to go.

FALLING IN LOVE

"Found poetry" from: The Magic Thief

I flung myself
Out the window
After him.
His hand was like a claw,
I gasped.
He stared up at me,
Eyes wide.
Blood dripped onto his face
"Let me go,"
He whispered.
"I will not let you fall."
He stared up at me,
His laugh was a high,
Scared sound.
I held him and then
He jerked
And I let him fall.

TRANSLUCENT SKIN

Translucent skin,
silhouettes of bone, grey with age
ribs aching with release.
A darkness, too thick to see through.
Head lowered,
windows all shuttered.

I peeked once.
Parted the drapes
that hung in heaps of shredded loneliness.
Plumes of dust enacted
plays of possibility.

Then there was light.
Pouring her sun kissed soul into my
outstretched arms.
I could do nothing but kneel,
tidal waves of gold
lapping up my arms,
painting my skin colours
found only after the rain's gone.

And then she turned.
The curtains flapped in the ghostly breeze.
Paralyzed,
her absence encased upon my chest.
The dark
turning me as cold
as stone.

. . . .

DRY EYELASHES AND DEAD SEABIRDS

The tattooist asks a question,
unwanted and inappropriate.
Suddenly,
my intimacies unravel into notice.
Profanity tastes thick and chunky in my mouth
as I bark my response, choking on tears:
Do you believe in unconditional lo--?

Sometimes (I tell myself)
I can still taste you
in the lip balm we used to share
but I know that you tasted nothing
of coconut or fruit punch, but instead of
dry eyelashes on my back before
the alarm went off.

Fumbling in the dark, you were something of a
solecism, a bird's wish
bone and I did not wish to break you.

You would not understand a heartache, a headache, a
soulache
like I do. Stretched skin on glass that tattooist asks:
Where are you? Where am I?

I see you silently crying in muddied theater,
sticky with popcorn and spilled sex
because he loved her.
But I'm ugly when I cuddle.
I excuse myself because all of a sudden,
I'm not crying about him anymore but
you, the chambers of my heart,
raw and empty.

There's this adhesive on my tongue
from trying to kiss it better.
It's not better.

The nursemaids look at her like she is a
stairway taken backwards.
Her tongue in my ear whispering, "do this gently"
while my voice is screaming:
you have the capability of being lost.

She puts on perfume, sculpting her
appendage into whatever he pleases,
but I know that you taste
nude underwater.

. . . .

Sometimes I think you're there
when you're not and
I say hi and you say
nothing back.

I remember you as things
pried from sunken fists,
coffee ring staining my trousers,
and the white places where you left me.
Two black eyeballs rolling through a dead seabird.
I lick the salt crystalizing under your nails.
I think god's suicide must be over because
I don't know how to lunatic like this--

I don't know how to love like this.

YOU AS I REMEMBER.

the perfume
from a rose,
overdue to fall.

BLINK

I wish time would pause
Just for a moment.
Wish I could touch time's shoulder,
Turn their attention to me and ask
"Could you spare a minute?"
Halt the pine needles that fall in and out
Of sunlight, glistening like fresh snow.
Cease the movement of tombstone shadows as noon
yawns.
Keep this feeling of your knee against mine and
The way the wind runs its fingers through your hair.
Delay the words about to fall from your mouth
Like dew from morning grass.
Please, oh please, don't end this graveside love.
Can I just have a few more seconds of enjoyment
To appreciate all the things I have learned are okay to
cherish:
The wind, the pine needles, the colour of brick, your
eyelashes
Before you
B l i n k
And tell me you can't love me anymore.

POLYAMORY

Will you find someone better than me?
Or worse, will you find someone just like me.

RECOVERING FROM YOU

How long did it take for me to realize
He was not my poetry?
The same time it takes for you to realize
The face in the mirror isn't your own.
The salt water on the shore won't stop
Pulling at your toes.
Felt dried up, sucked out,
A vacuum filled space…
But how can emptiness *feel*
Like it's taking over my body?
I feel empty heavy in my chest,
Wallowing in the dip of my collar bone,
The cold seizing my breath away
icannotbreatheicannotbreatheicannot
breathe.
How long did it take for me to realize
He was not my poetry?
I found a rock on the beach
Holding his hand.

Letting it go to backtrack- and there it was:
Perfect hole through the middle,
Raved about it for days,
Thought I ought to give it to him
All wrapped up because he would know
That I like him more than this perfect rock
With a hole through the middle.
The next day
It broke.

MOVED ON

Have I moved on?
I don't even know what that means anymore.
Moved on… to where?
Is there a place that can take my limp heart,
Thread the edges back together so that
They're no longer frayed and torn?
Do they take cash or card?
Are you supposed to leave a tip?
There's a snag in the stitching,
Will they be willing to refund?

DESSERT

Brought your love to dinner, almost as an afterthought.

THE NEWS I HEARD WHEN THEY LET ME OUT OF SUBACUTE

You nearly jumped off a bridge.
How do you expect me to feel?
I heard about it today, they had just let me out.
My mind was still on plasticy beds and sloppily made
meals.
The very day they took me to the hospital they took you
too.
I feel like I want to be mad. But then again, I was doing
the same.
Staring into that dark abyss of hopelessness.
Yours was over a river, mine was the reflection in the
mirror.
Am I too fragile for you to hold?
I don't know if I can keep myself together so how do you
expect
Me to keep you from venturing over the edge again?
I feel so lost and I don't know how to tell you that
I'm scared.
I'm scared that it's not going to get better, ever.
I'm scared cause all I think about is getting out of the
house once I'm 18 and
Cutting myself up into pretty pink bows.
You stare at your phone and are immersed in all the people
you're taking care of.

. . . .

. . . .

But I'm right next to you writing this poem. I'm right next
to you.
I know you love a lot and that's why you spend so much
time online.
I just wish you would love me a lot too.
Makes me feel so lonely. And that's the worst:
Loneliness. The absolute worst. Hideously porous
I do not know where it stops and I begin.

. . . .

OFFLINE

I sit in silence.
Phone: a black hole
Through which my words
(If I ever had the courage to speak)
Would be sucked into
The black maw of your unanswering.
My mother broke her foot.
Oh. I hope she's okay.
No "i miss you" no "how are you doing"
No interest in my life now that you're no longer in it.
I'm with someone else now.
Did you know that?
Would you care?
All feelings for you shriveled up inside me
That night after you said "let's just be friends"
But you said you still loved me.
Do you still love me?
Now that I've come out of the cistem,
Do you still love me?
I crave apology.
A single goddamn apology.

. . . .

You turned me away and left me to the
Swarming masses of strangers
And said that I'd be alright
While you check your watch and
Absentmindedly wave goodbye
To make it to a party.
You were all I had.
I told you that. I said:
You
Are
All
I
Have.
(please don't leave me).
My sisters were right.
All the nasty things they said
Were right, I guess because you didn't stay with me.
I needed a friend and now
You don't text.

. . . .

WHEN DEPRESSION HAS TURNED YOU INTO A CRUSTY COUCH POTATO @ 4:48 AM AND YOU COULDN'T GIVE 2 FUCKS ABOUT IT BECAUSE

it was sort of nice
doing nothing.
all of the time.

SOUR

Can you tell by looking in my eyes?
Can you hear by listening to my heart?
Can you taste it by drinking in my presence?
Can you smell it by sniffing my skin?
I am sour. Molten, porous, something yellow
That shouldn't be
Yellow.
I don't know how to do anything besides
Mash my hands together,
Pulpy mess I make
Of our love.
Do your eyes sting?
Does your tongue recoil?
I am not a sweet drink meant for straw-sipping.

OTHERWISE

How do I tell you I've been feeling otherwise?

WITH(OUT) YOU

I must decide what I want,
Do I want him, or something else?
Something more?
But what is more if it's not this?
Is there a next for me?
I keep thinking there'll be an afterwards but
He's here spinning forever on his tongue:
We don't have time for these
Broken distractions.
You must decide what you want and if you do not know
If there'll be a next or not, what choice do you have?
Will you give it all up for a future you haven't met yet?
You know me, so why do you want to leave?
I don't know, I don't know.

I AM NOT YOUR FOREVER

This isn't forever.
This is all temporary,
The pain, the passion,
The love. That's what
They taught me in therapy
And I realize now that you
Are not my forever.
You are not my everything
Because you cannot give me
The world because you can't
Give me your heart. Your name.
You were an escape from the loneliness
A break in the emptiness
But even you will
Be gone soon. I'll leave in the fall
And you won't be able to run after me
Because you can't run.
You can't even walk towards me
Without falling to your knees.
I've given you my all but there's too much
Of you still in pieces to give me your
Everything. There's not enough scraps
To scavenge together for even yourself.

You are not my all and
You are not my everything.
The only reason why I haven't left you yet
Is because I think that you believe I am your forever.
And I would very much like to avoid
Breaking your heart into any more
Scattered pieces.
Forgive me, this is my first break up
Poem and the only poem of mine
That you will never read.

NOTICE MY LEAVING

I think I fell in love with you.
Tumbled and tripped over awkward first kisses
And tangled legs under covers.
I loved your lips on mine and the way you'd whisper into
the bedsheets.
I realized soon that there was this space between our kisses
where I knew you'd forgotten about me.
I would tickle the back of your neck or graze your earlobe
with my teeth in attempts to draw you back.
To me. *Am I here for you? Can you see me, I'm right here.*
Eventually you'd turn back and I'd get lost in those eyes of
yours and forget your forgetting.
But it would happen again. That awful pause where I
couldn't for the life of me figure out what was going on in
that little head of yours. I've gotten tired of it.
I think that after a while I left you there on the ground,
fumbling around with the ghost of me
And I started to get up, to walk away. I feel the passion
draining and I no longer crave to
Kiss you like I used to. I've picked myself up, left love
behind and walked on without you.

· · · ·

But you don't know that, do you? You haven't realized
that I'm no longer in love with you,
Rather I'm somewhere far far away, getting ever farther,
looking over my shoulder at those oblivious eyes and the
love that couldn't pay enough attention to me
To notice my leaving.

LAST AND FIRST KISS

It was something brusque, abrupt, there and then gone.
His mouth was on hers, bruising and impregnated with
passion. Urgency dripping from every pore. His hands
yanked at a face he'd found so beautiful, once. He had
thought her beautiful, hadn't he? Fingers searched the deep
crevasses for answers.

Her drabby flabs swished within their fist-tight collision
and her rattling chest struggled to breathe through the
squashed noses, snot, and tears. Teeth impaled his lips as
she tried to drag his blubbering mouth into her own. She
used her tongue to scoop more of him inside her.
Spoonfuls. Bit by bit. Piece by piece. Fill her, fill her.
He broke her clenching grip, spat her saliva out of himself
in disgust. She tasted porous, oozing, leakage. He hurried
towards the open train, stooped and aghast by their fifty-
seven years of pounding sex, adverted gazes, cold nights.
His coat trailed on the ground in a sloppy mess and she felt
she ought to tell him off for it. His skin too, hung off his
skeletal frame in curtains, billowing in the breeze from the
tunnel. Her automating voice instructed him to carry his
flapping flesh so as to not make a fool of himself, while
mostly hacking into a handkerchief. *Carry your age, old
man. That's it. Don't you be bringing it home either. Leave it
on the doorstep and I'll make sure to take it out in the
morning.*

She didn't want it. If this was love, she wanted nothing to do with it at all. It was ugly. Short and pimply with bad breath. Its sweat got all over her skin in an uncomfortable smear and its hands were spindly and uncoordinated, palpating her nib of a breast like a bike pump. Like maybe if it just squeezed more, she'd inflate with passion. Its tongue too, when not on her lips, was greasing the hollow of her neck and filling her ears with bubbly saliva that made popping sounds. She had tried to shout, get it off her, but her cries were muffled by the horrifying noises it made. Groaning, huffing, hissing like some animal, the kind people kill because they feel like cleaning the world up a little. She had to stand there, squeezing her eyes shut, holding her breath, keeping her mouth closed because god forbid, if she'd open it just a peep it'd slither inside her and make her taste the most awful of things. She had to withstand what felt like hours of this love. By the end of it she was limping with exhaustion, dripping with disgust, and radiating with one clear determination. She would live her whole life killing all of this, this love that lurked in the drainpipes and alleyways of the darkest and dirtiest parts of the world. The stuff that ruined people's lives, she'd rid of it before it stained their skin too.

. . . .

FUCKED UP

I want to be funny.
Crack jokes like it's second nature,
Be able to make a room swell with laughter.
I want to be dependable.
The one people go to talk to
When they're feeling blue or black or some sort of grey.
I want to be trusted
With secrets they tell me.
Keep them locked in a little chest under my shoes.
I want to be likeable.
Quirky and cute and perfect.
Mostly, I just want to have friends
But I can't make my brain say the words that will make
that happen.
Instead, I mumble something about the things we have in
common under my breath but you think I'm scoffing at
something you said and your chin tilts away in modest
disgust and I know you hate me now. My fingers fumble
over the spines of books while you strut off in indignation
and I'm trailing after you like a goddamn puppy craving
attention and you slow your pace because you realize that
I'm just a sad sight. All I'm thinking is how desperately I
want to go back and make it right again.

. . . .

Was it ever right?
Must have been right at some point then I came along and

fucked everything up.

Now you can't even bear the thought of looking at me
and what if, what if, what if I mess it up again with this
boy?
This boy in the adorable jellyfish shirt and cream-coloured
glasses
and he realizes what a

fucked up

person I am
and decides that he doesn't want that in his life
and blocks my number and I don't even realize
that he's blocked it (or I do but don't consciously
acknowledge it).
and I keep texting with someone who isn't even listening,
isn't even there,
isn't even *there* then I'm truly and absolutely

fucked.

HOMEROOM

He's over there at the table.
Somewhere, a few seats away,
But it feels like he's farther.
On a steamship with all the
Bells and
Whistles and I'm on the dock,
Looking at my reflection in the
Murky water below thinking:
Why can't you just jump?

ROCK JUMPING

Salt in hair
Sloshing.
White bits of foam
Surface: oily
Feel its sheen on your toes
Still submerged
Rock rears back
Lunges towards you
Gnashes your palms
Can't tell if it's blood or ocean
Dripping down your arms.
Blades of light piercing,
Puncturing waves
Is this where it happens?
Between the cries of seabirds
And blinking crabs?
You pull knees to chest
Cradle mauled hands
Look over the edge.
For all it was worth
Was it worth all this?
Gingerly tiptoeing across
Jagged teeth

Wincing when soft flesh
Of the arch slits open
She had told you
Bring shoes.
But how could you
She doesn't get it
The naked skin, the
Raw rock,
The places they meet
Sloshing
Back and forth between
Pain and
"I'm alive."
You think you hear her voice then
Somewhere hovering
Just below the lip.
You curl your toes over
Shutting her up
Then you fall
Brusque air sipping
Water off your back
Flash of betrayal:
Thought the clouds would catch me
Consumed again
Black maw of the deep

. . . .

Could you sink?
Could you sink farther?
Imagining spongy sand
Cool caress of darkness
Would this be death?
Lungs constrict
Your heart plunges
Feet kick up
Air.

. . . .

DARK SHORES

Lips cracking with salt,
My fingers grasp for pearl truths
Among your dark shores.

HUNGRY GHOST

Clocking and churning
Teeth against metal.
Chains spindling downwards,
Cracked spines, mechanical
Vertebrae vibrating.

So much noise in my head…

Is he real?
Hungry ghost,
Is he real yet?

Sombre shadows thick
Like butter on my skin.
Sinking into the pores of my
Being. Gears cackling
In the background,
Tongue caught in the wires.

So much death in my head.

Are you real?
Beautiful stranger,
Are you real yet?

Dried ink along my jaw-
Bone, fingers itching inside
Of sockets, sparking
Wet electricity,
Rocking on heels tied up with cords.

Oh, so much love on my mind.

Am I real?
Hungry, beautiful self,
Am I real yet?

MONARCH

He spent an hour last night singing to me.
Over the phone it was hard sometimes to hear his voice
over the guitar
Or over the music from the living room.

He came in and ruffled my hair and then left.
I wanted to follow but there were already people walking
him out.
And, and, and my legs can't move. I regret everything.

My thoughts are like auburn pine needles,
Fluttering hesitantly in the sunlight, cautious of falling too
Fast for him.

I've only had this feeling once before:
Standing on top of the world, toes curled over the edge
The wind, the *before* I drop and fall towards the water.

My eyelids feel like wet butterfly wings:
Struggling to open, flailing across the grass,
Tired of crying for someone I haven't met yet.

STUCK

His chin tilts back as he sings and lips
crack a smile and I want to say I ... you.
His head in my lap, my fingers lazily
tracing circles around his forehead,
the arch of his nose and I want to say:
do you know how much I ... you?
Half listening to whatever it is he's saying
my lips pursed against the back of his neck,
I want to murmur all different ways
I've fallen in ... with him against his skin.
The pressure of it seems unbearable at times.
L gets hoisted up my throat but the jagged corner
scratches the inside of my esophagus.
Wetness wells under my tongue and
I can't tell if it's blood or saliva.
O gets stuck somewhere in the middle and I have to
cough into my elbow to dislodge its stubbornness.
V is hauled up backwards, arms catching,
grabbing a hold of whatever crack it can jam its fingers
into.

E is just a bitch. All legs, arms, and ass.
Refuses to make eye contact and
sticks out its tongue as it's shoved up my throat.
All the letters are on my tongue.
You lean in and press against my lips.
My mouth opens, tongues touch.
I hope you can taste all the words
that I have been too scared to tell you.
Words like:
I.
Love.
and
You.

CAN I HAVE YOUR NUMBER

Can I have your phone number?
Was probably the bravest thing I ever asked.
Of course, it's not nearly anything
Remotely
Close to the questions I wanted to ask.
(Can I hold your hand?
Will you read my poetry?
Can we be friends?)

You like my music
I like you.

- *is that alright?*

I DON'T MIND HOW YOU KISS ME

Your hand brings mine towards your lips.
Glasses slip and fog, your
Eye meets mine, a deep pool of swirling
Questions and answers, all tinted with chocolate
Milk and the sunlight through birch trees.
I'm worried that my palm is clammy but you raise my
hand and
Your lips part slightly and I forget about
My hand,
My feet,
My breath.
As I imagine the kiss to come,
Your lips only a little cracked,
Softly pink, the shape of your mouth
As you kiss my---
Suddenly, you jerk and teeth sink into my fingers,
I bite my tongue in surprise, tears well in my eyes from
The pain and effort it takes to keep smiling
While you try to eat my hand.

THIS IS HOW I WANT YOU.

Sea of teenagers foaming by the mouth,
Drenched in odor and swaths of cologne.
A red t-shirt, a chin cast awry…
This is when I found you.

Snippets of stories and song lyrics,
Scribbled on hotel paper and a
Triangular stone.
This is how I found you.

Morning sun soaks the blinds,
Caught in the honeycomb ribs.
The pulse of shared breath…
This is when I want you.

Bending down nearly nose to nose
With a skulled creature long since decayed,
Withered and wanderlust...
This is why I want you.

Willow tree laden with autumn and
Hunched over like an old man---
Whispering chimes and candle wax bark…
This is where I want you.

. . . .

Sprawled across twisted sheets,
Arms askew--- the bottom bit of a bird's nest
Gently pulling away from the body…
This is how I want you.

SOME SORT OF LOVE LETTER

Acorns crack under your white boots, scuffed around the edges, worn with love.
I only hope it's been my love that's brushed against your sole/soul.
Beneath that messily stitched heart that you wear on your sleeve, there's something so, so beautiful it makes my eyes ache.
Candy cane taste around my teeth, visions of Christmas with this poem's rhyme lingering on the cusp of my lip while you sit below, cross legged. That smile in your eyes, I want to kiss that smile.
Can I kiss your eyes?
Devil, wrap your spiked tongue around my throat and keep my mind off the boy with green hair, for he is like an intoxicating drug that I can't seem to get enough of.
Eventually, the nervousness that pinches the inside of my stomach and rattles between my ribs will subside like the ocean tide, am I right? Tell me I'm right because I don't know how much longer I can pretend I don't want to jump up and smash my lips into yours.

Flossing my toes with the words you whisper into my bed
sheets when you think I'm not listening (I am I am I am)
forgetting how to use my mouth to respond.
Ghost, phantom limb, phantom love you are to me.
There's this absence when we're not together that pulls at
my being, there should be something here but where are
you?
Have you thought of me today? I'd like to think so.
Ice this fire that roars across my collarbone and flares up
my cheeks. Damn you for making me blush like I've been
leaning ever so closely towards a blazing bonfire under the
twilight evening.
Just once can I claim you as mine? I don't want to get used
to this feeling of protectiveness over you because it will
swell against my better judgement and I may punch
somebody's teeth down their throat for getting in your
way. But the idea is sweet and I can't resist thinking it.
Kiss me again. And again (And again).
Lose yourself in the early hours of the morning, fingers
entwined with my hair at the nape of my neck, we can
sleep in all day, every day.

Missing parts of myself, I never knew I had, are hidden in the crook of your neck, the spaces between your fingers, tucked away under your chin. I grab at them greedily, marveling at their frailty, at all the delicate corners, edges. Piece me back together, slowly fill the emptiness.

Nightmares galloping through your head, come, let's learn to braid horse hair and tame the horrors that once haunted us.

Over and over, I want to fall in love with you.

Please take off your shoes, let me undo your laces, your mistakes, your eyelashes. Let tears splash against your glasses, don't worry I'll clean them later. You'll see clearly again soon, and it doesn't have to be now.

Quit questioning the way the leaves flutter and fall from the tree, reach inside my mouth and pull up the foliage of my being, mushy brown at the edges from slipping into puddles on sidewalks. Hold my soul in your hands, this is me, this is me and ask yourself instead: is this what I want? Remind yourself how to let the past go, release that death clutch around the red balloon. Doesn't it look peaceful up there with the birds? Learn to kiss again with a mouth slightly ajar, slightly open, slightly softer than those you've experienced.

Smothering my face into your pillow, is it strange that I can't stop thinking of you? My lungs are puffy with exhaustion, hyperventilation rasping my insides raw but my face is buried in your pillow and I can breathe again. After so many nights of suffocation, I can breathe again.
Twirl into my arms, I want to hold you in meadows of dandelions because I know those are your favorite.
Unfold this tattered envelope of a life and transform all my rotten bits into pretty pink poetry.
Voices cascade like rivers of doubt around my shins, I am knee deep in embarrassment because I don't know how to love you like I want too.
Washed ashore are the crumpled shells of who we used to be, this salt crusted under your nails remind me of how far we will go together, wading through the oceans wherever you wish to go.
Examined, I've been poked and prodded, flopping like a beached goldfish under fluorescent lights. They pick at my scales and pry my mask off inch by inch, exposing the naked and puckered flesh underneath.
Yesterday you…
Zzz i'm getting sleepy, it's 3 am i'm going to bed now, i love you.

· · · ·

THANK YOU

The boy in the jellyfish shirt
Asked if I wanted to play cards.
He probably doesn't know how much
That saved my life.

ACKNOWLEDGEMENTS

This wouldn't be possible without the support of a whole heck ton of people. The first person I'd like to thank would be Richard Braithwaite, my high school English teacher who called me a poet even before I knew that what I was writing was poetry. Second would be Jaime Johnson, my rock climbing partner who reminded me that rock climbing is more about falling than it is about reaching the top, but we continue to do it because when we summit, the feeling is ineffable. I'd like to thank their children Summit and Eli for making me laugh during a time when I was lost and scared of myself.

Thank you to my sisters: Josie, Emma, Bryn, and Claire and their wonderful partners who make me feel like I belong. My parents for trusting me always. My friends: Martha & Finn Gleichmann, Dominic & Jonah Wallbridge, Benjamin Mendrin, Levin Neumann, Hisham Kanaan, Clara Velasco Ullenhag, and Maria Haddad. Thank you to all my English teachers and role models: Molly VanCleave, Karen Lombard, Mireille Neil, Morgan Anderson, Tracy Ramberg, Honor McElroy, James Brown, Keri Nickles, and Cara Forty. A hundred hugs and kisses to my soulmate Quinn Scanlon who knows all my darkest parts and chooses to love me nonetheless.
The editing, format, layout, cover design, and publication

of this book was made possible through donations made by the following friends and family. I'm eternally grateful, you made my dream become a reality.

Steven & Anne, Rick & Bonnie Johnson, Genevieve Johnson, Debbie Rolin & Petra Harvey, Rhyan Schaub, Kim Wolfenden, James Housego & Malia Bohdaine, Judy & Peter Gray, Martina & John Magnan, Natascha Magnan, Colin & Frauka Gleichmann, Collin Gruenwald, Jen Jane, Kelly Mou, Paola San-Martini, Joe Swinehart, Jessica & Jasion Levitt, Karen Lombard, Mireille Neil, Elloise Engel & Charlie Bowels, Lynn & John Gaylord, Miriah Kellison, Kristi Darzynkiewicz and Ritch Viola.

ABOUT THE AUTHOR

Aspen Harvey is a non-binary poet who grew up in Asia, the Middle East, Africa, and graduated high school in Oregon. They are 18 years old and have a moth tattoo on their left wrist in association with the butterfly movement for those who struggle with self-harm (but moths are way cooler). They work as a youth rock climbing coach at a local bouldering gym and enjoy swimming, hiking, laying in the rain, junk journaling, and thrift shopping. And of course writing poetry.